MW00893123

The mission of Wolgemuth & Hyatt, Publishers, Inc. is to publish and distribute books that lead individuals toward:

- A personal faith in the one true God: Father, Son, and Holy Spirit;

- A lifestyle of practical discipleship; and

- A worldview that is consistent with the historic, Christian faith.

Moreover, the company endeavors to accomplish this mission at a reasonable profit and in a manner which glorifies God and serves His Kingdom.

© 1990 by Mary Pride. All rights reserved.
Illustrations © 1990 by Wolgemuth & Hyatt Publishers, Inc.
Published October, 1990. First Edition
Printed in the United States of America
96 95 94 93 92 91 90   8 7 6 5 4 3 2 1

No part of this publication may be reproduced, stored in a retrieval system, or transmitted in any form by any means, electronic, mechanical, photocopy, recording, or otherwise, without the prior written permission of the publisher, except for brief quotations in critical reviews or articles.

Illustrations by Vic Lockman.

Wolgemuth & Hyatt, Publishers, Inc.
1749 Mallory Lane, Suite 110, Brentwood, Tennessee 37027.

Library of Congress Cataloging-in-Publication Data

Pride, Mary
    Too many chickens : old wise tales / Mary Pride. — 1st ed.
      p. cm. — (Old wise tales)
    Summary: Farmer Apple's pigs feel that there are too many chickens depleting the corn supply.
    ISBN 1-56121-010-2 : $8.95
    [1. Chickens—Fiction. 2. Pigs—Fiction. 3. Greed—Fiction.
    4. Population—Fiction. 5. Farm life—Fiction.] I. Title.
    II. Series.
    P27.P93428To   1990
    [Fic]—dc20   90-43861
                                        CIP
                                        AC

TOO MANY CHICKENS

by
Mary Pride

Wolgemuth & Hyatt, Publishers, Inc.
Brentwood, Tennessee

Life was easy on Farmer Apple's farm.

The pigs rooted happily
in their pen.

The chickens scratched for the corn Farmer Apple's little girl threw them each day.

The goats and ducks and other animals played together nice[ly]

. . . most of the time.

Until one day, the biggest pig of all decided he wanted MORE CORN.

He saw that Farmer Apple's girl fed corn to both the pigs and the chickens. The chickens got the grain and the pigs got the corncobs.

This isn't fair, Big Pig thought to himself. *I am bigger than all these chickens put together! I deserve to have more corn than they do.*

So he called a meeting of the pigs.
"We need more corn!" Big Pig grunted.
All the other pigs agreed that they needed more corn.

"But where can we get more corn?" a little pig asked.

"From the chickens!" Big Pig replied. "They are eating too much corn. From now on, the chickens will have to share their corn with the pigs."

So from that day on, whenever Farmer Apple's girl left the farmyard,

the pigs made the chickens bring them half their corn.

The chickens got thinner.
The pigs got fatter.
But Big Pig still wasn't happy.
He wanted MORE corn!

So Big Pig called another meeting.

"What we have here is TOO MANY CHICKENS!" he said. "Too many chickens eating too much corn! There isn't enough for the rest of us."

All the fat pigs agreed that there were too many thin chickens.

"But what can we do about it?" the little pig asked. "We can't just ask the chickens to leave!"

"That's right," Big Pig said. "Farmer Apple would not be happy if anything happened to his chickens. But if they didn't lay so many eggs, he might get rid of them himself. And besides, with fewer eggs there would be fewer chickens!"

"The hens have to stop having so many chicks!"
All the other pigs agreed that this was a fine idea.

Soon the word was passed through the farmyard.
"There isn't enough corn for all of us because
there are TOO MANY CHICKENS. It is the duty
of every hen to stop laying so many eggs."

At first the hens were upset.

But then they got used to not laying so many eggs. They noticed that they kept their figures longer.

They noticed that fewer chicks meant more time to gossip with their friends.

Soon the hens had formed a Two-Egg Club.

Every hen in the farmyard was a member except
Mrs. Pinfeather.

"I don't care!" said Mrs. Pinfeather. "God made hens to lay eggs. Besides, I love baby chicks!"

The pigs were happy that the hens had stopped laying so many eggs. But the other hens were very angry with Mrs. Pinfeather. "What right does she have to use up so much corn?" they asked each other.

The biggest hen called a meeting.
She said, "What we have here is TOO MANY CHICKENS!
Too many chickens eating too much corn!
There isn't enough for the rest of us.
Mrs. Pinfeather and her family have to GO!"

So Mrs. Pinfeather and her family had to leave the farm.

They were surprised at how big the world was. And how full it was of corn!

For several days they stayed in the cornfield, eating and eating. They stopped being thin.

The little ones played tag among the cornstalks.

On the fourth day, Mrs. Pinfeather smelled something. She asked her oldest son, "Winky, will you fly up on top of the cornstalks and see what is making that smell?"

But Winky was too fat to fly up that high.

Neither could his sisters, Blinky, Pinky, and Minky, nor his brothers, Dinky, Linky, and Stinky.

"All right," said Mrs. Pinfeather. "Winky, you get on my back. Dinky, you stand on him, and tell me what is making that smell."

So Winky jumped up on Mrs. Pinfeather's back, and Dinky jumped up on top of Winky. But Dinky still couldn't see over the top of the corn.

"I see that two chicks aren't enough," said Mrs. Pinfeather. "Linky, you stand on Dinky." So Linky jumped up on Dinky. But Linky still couldn't see over the top of the corn.

"All right," said Mrs. Pinfeather. "There's always a way when a family sticks together. Stinky, you stand on Linky. Blinky, you stand on Stinky. Pinky, you stand on Blinky. Minky, you stand on Pinky, and when you see what is making that smell, SING OUT!"

So Stinky jumped up on Linky
and Blinky jumped up on Stinky
and Pinky jumped up on Blinky
and Minky jumped up on Pinky

and Minky saw what was making that smell.
    It was a prairie fire!
    And it was headed right for Farmer Apple's farm!

The animals in the farmyard were so lazy and fat from eating too much corn that none of them even noticed the smell. None of them could be bothered to see what it was. And, even if they had looked, none of them was tall enough to look over the cornstalks and see the fire so far away.

Mrs. Pinfeather knew the farm animals were in trouble. So she and Winky, Dinky, Linky, Stinky, Blinky, Pinky, and Minky ran straight to the farm. "Wake up, everyone!" they cheeped. "A fire! A fire is headed this way!"

All the animals woke up in a hurry.

What could they do? A fire would burn the farm all up!
And Farmer Apple had taken his family to town for the day!

Big Pig was the first to move. "Come with me, you pigs," he grunted. "We have to dig a ring around the farm with our snouts. You goats, bring water from the well. Chickens, dip your wings in the water and wet down the barn roof."

Everyone got busy. They did just as Big Pig had said.

Mrs. Pinfeather and her family worked harder than anyone else. Working as a team, they wet down not only the barn roof, but the henhouse roof as well.

The farm was saved!

After the fire was out, Big Pig called another meeting.
This time, everyone came, not just the pigs.

"We pigs are sorry we were so piggy about the corn," he said. "We see now that we were wrong. We did not have too many chickens on this farm. We had barely enough!"

Everyone laughed.

And Mrs. Pinfeather and her chicks laughed the loudest!